THE GARDEN OF ABDUL GASAZI

Written and Illustrated by CHRIS VAN ALLSBURG

HOUGHTON MIFFLIN COMPANY BOSTON

To Lisa

Library of Congress Cataloging in Publication Data

Van Allsburg, Chris.
The garden of Abdul Gasazi.

SUMMARY: When the dog he is caring for runs away
from Alan into the forbidden garden of a retired dog-
hating magician, a spell seems to be cast over the
contrary dog.

[1. Magicians—Fiction. 2. Dogs—Fiction]
I. Title.
PZ7.V266Gar   [E]   79-17610
ISBN 0-395-27804-X

Printed in the United States of America.
Lib. of C. Card No. 79-016844

H IO 9

THE GARDEN OF ABDUL GASAZI

Six times Miss Hester's dog Fritz had bitten dear cousin Eunice. So when Miss Hester received an invitation to visit Eunice she was not surprised to read "P.S., Please leave your dog home." On the day of her visit Miss Hester asked young Alan Mitz to stay with Fritz and give him his afternoon walk.

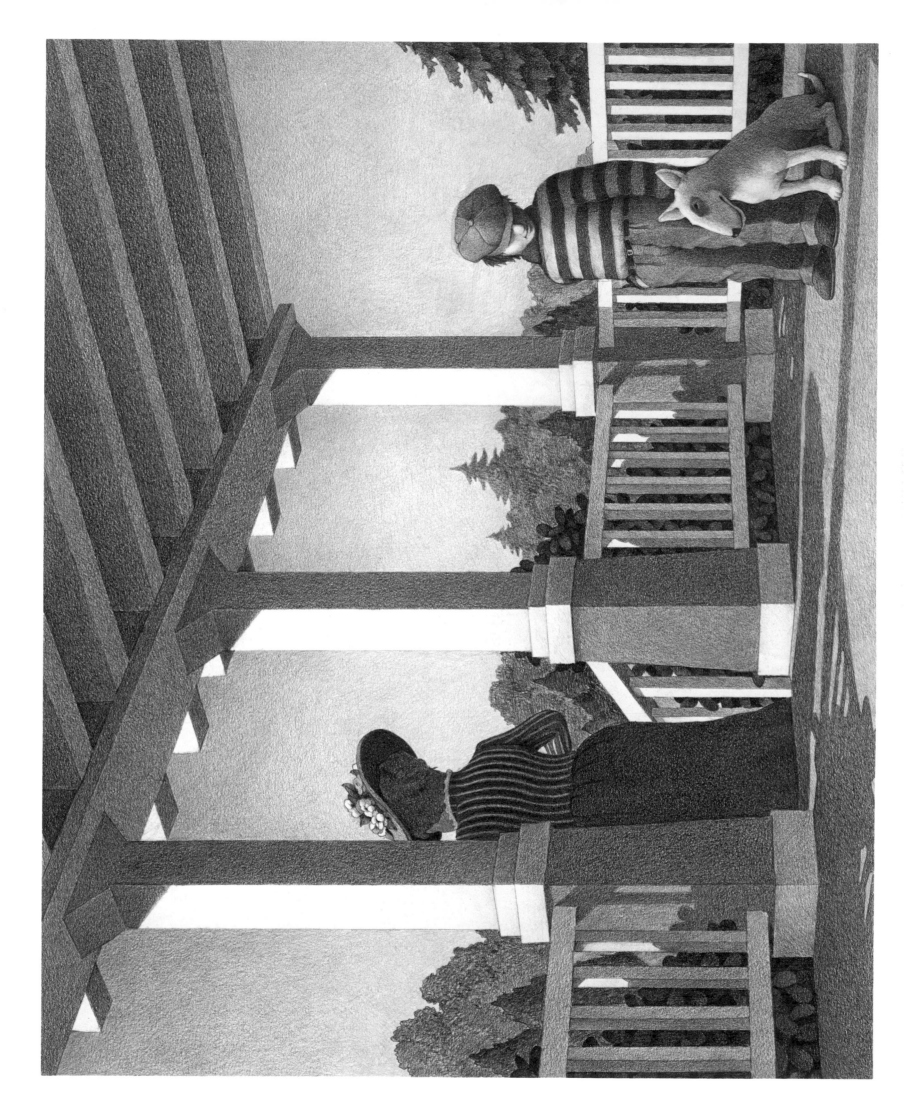

As soon as Miss Hester left, Fritz ran into the parlor. He loved to chew on the chairs and shake the stuffing out of the pillows. But Alan was ready. All morning long he kept Fritz from sinking his sharp little teeth into the furniture. Finally the dog gave up and fell asleep, exhausted. Alan took a nap, too, but first he hid his hat under his shirt, hats being one of Fritz's favorite things to chew.

An hour later Alan quickly awoke when Fritz gave him a bite on the nose. The bad-mannered dog was ready for his afternoon walk. Alan fastened Fritz's leash and the dog dragged him out of the house. Walking along, they discovered a small white bridge at the side of the road. Alan decided to let Fritz lead the way across.

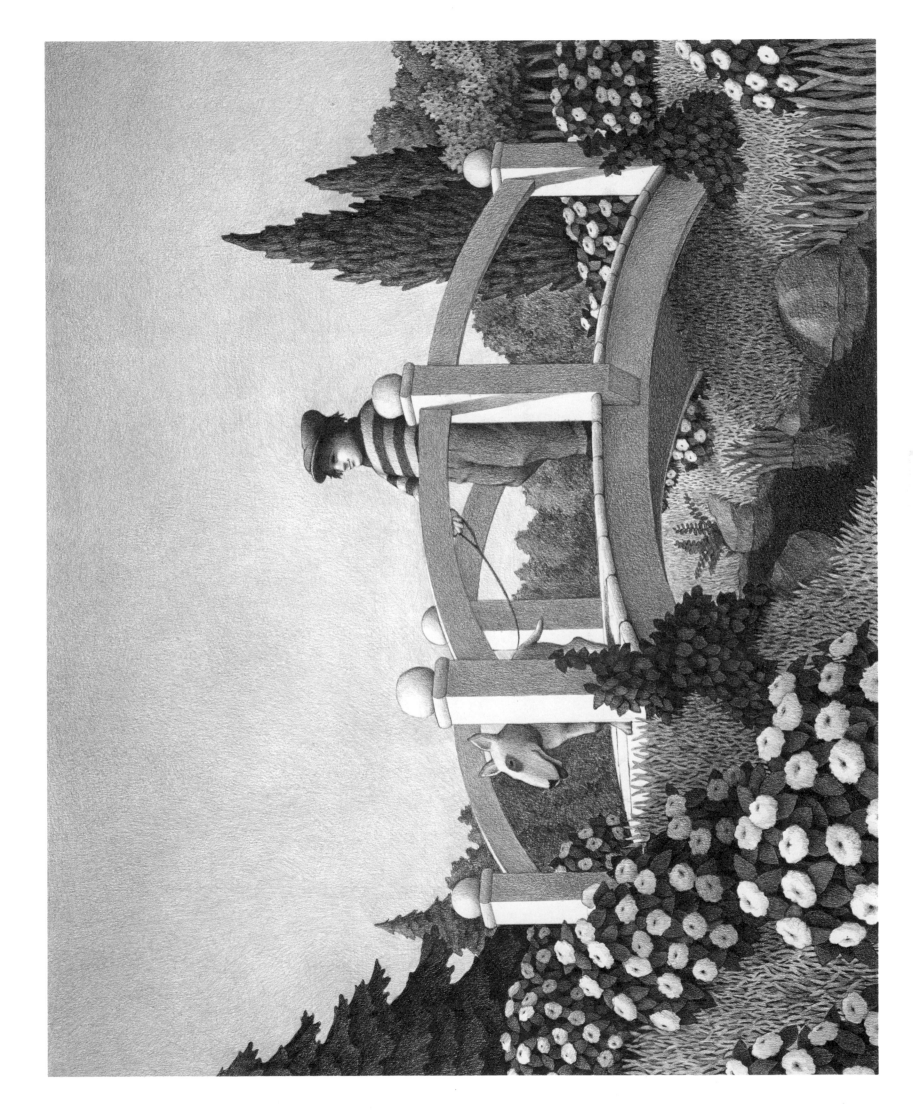

Some distance beyond the bridge Alan stopped to read a sign. It said: ABSOLUTELY, POSITIVELY NO DOGS ALLOWED IN THIS GARDEN. At the bottom it was signed: ABDUL GASAZI, RETIRED MAGICIAN. Behind the sign stood a vine-covered wall with an open doorway. Alan took the warning quite seriously. He turned to leave, but as he did, Fritz gave a tremendous tug and snapped right out of his collar. He bolted straight ahead through the open door, with Alan running right behind.

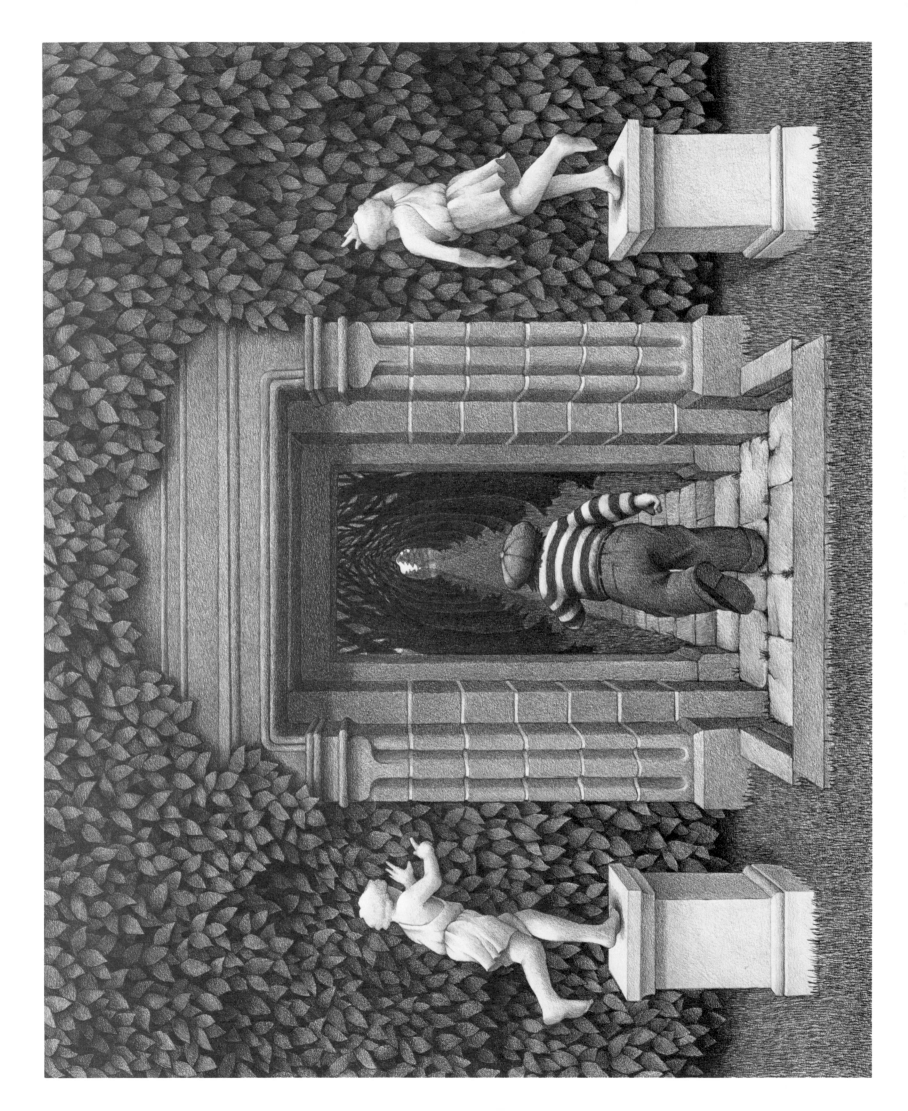

"Fritz, stop, you bad dog!" cried Alan, but the dog simply ignored him. Down shadowed paths and across sunlit lawns they raced, deeper and deeper into the garden. Finally, Alan drew close enough to grab hold of Fritz. But as he reached out he slipped and fell. Fritz barked with laughter as he galloped out of sight. Alan slowly picked himself up. He knew he had to find Fritz before Mr. Gasazi discovered him. Bruised and tired, he hurried off in the dog's direction.

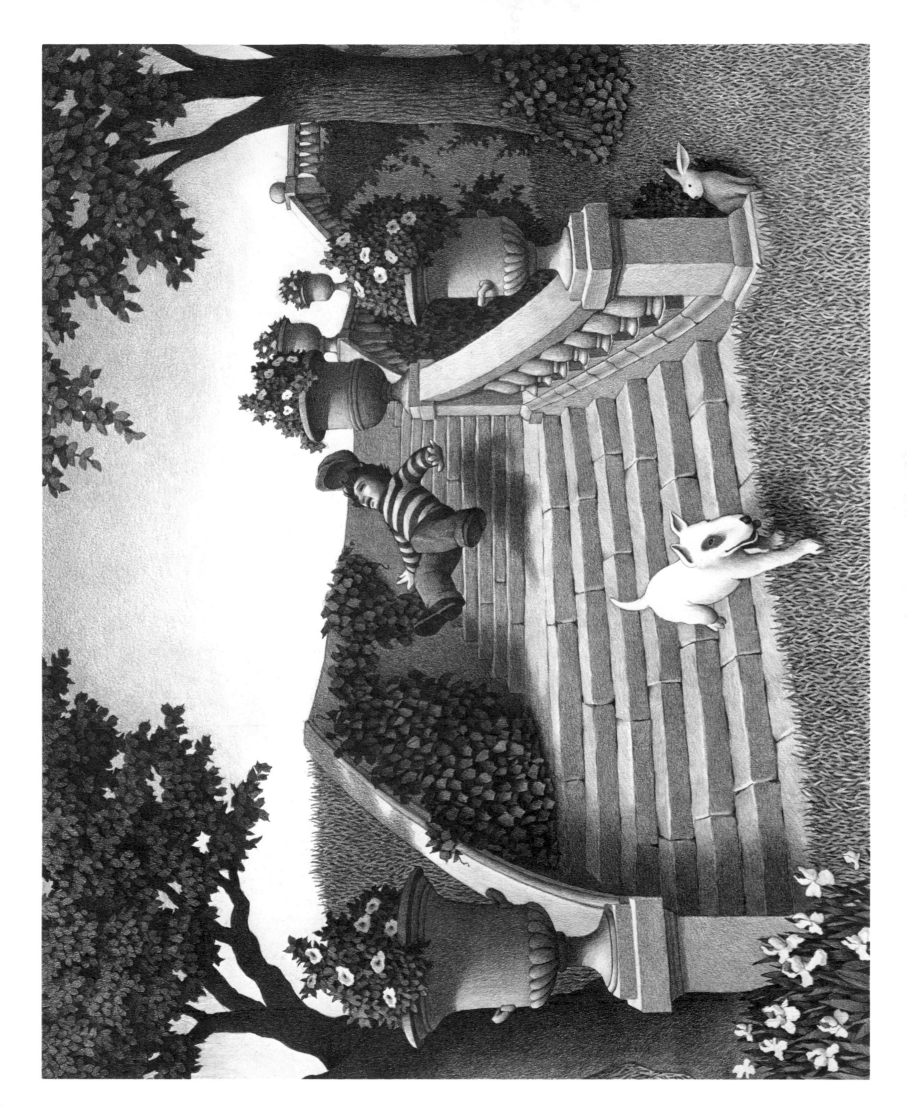

After a long search Alan was ready to give up. He was afraid he might never find Fritz. But then he came upon fresh dog prints. Slowly he followed Fritz's tracks along a path that led into a forest. The dirt path ended and a brick walk began. There were no more tracks to follow, but Alan was certain that Fritz must be just ahead.

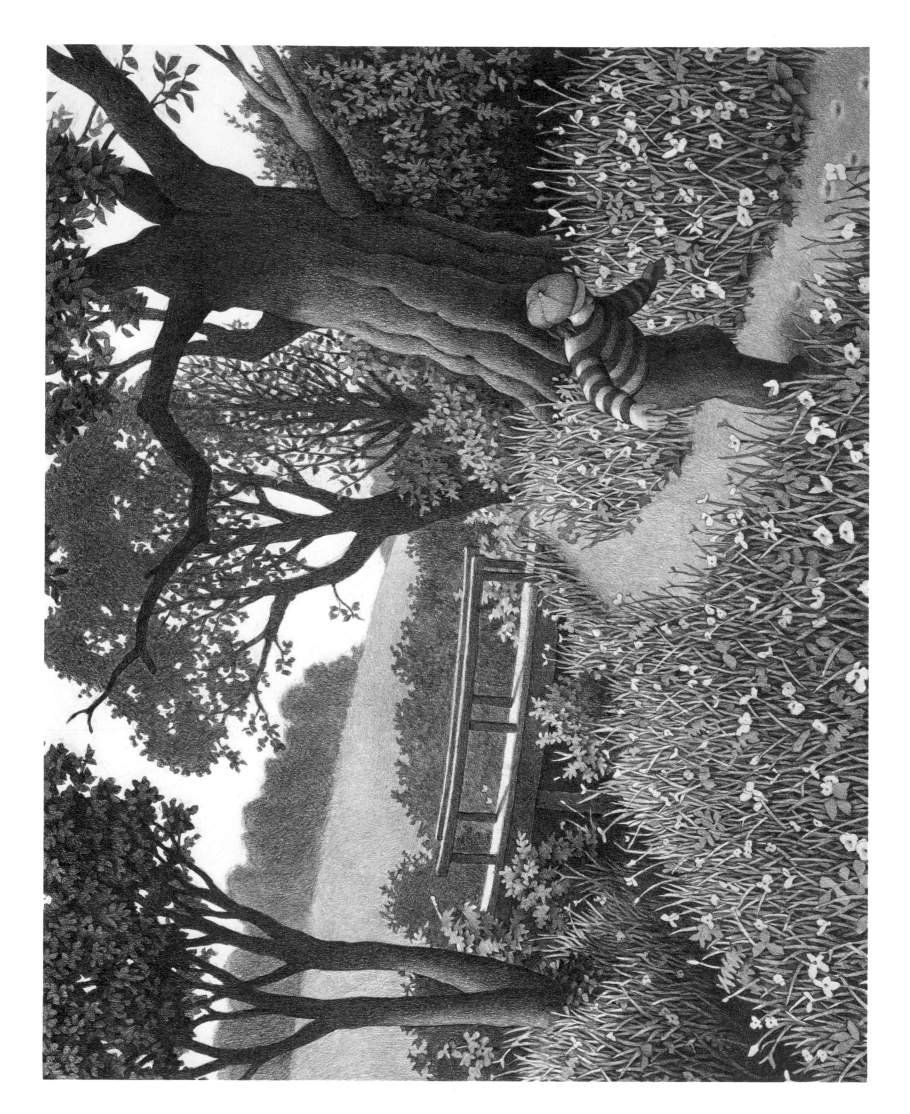

Alan started running. In front of him he could see a clearing in the forest. As he came dashing out of the woods he stopped as quickly as if he had run up against a wall. For there, in front of him, stood a truly awesome sight. It was the house of Gasazi. Alan nervously climbed the great stairs, convinced Fritz had come this way and been captured.

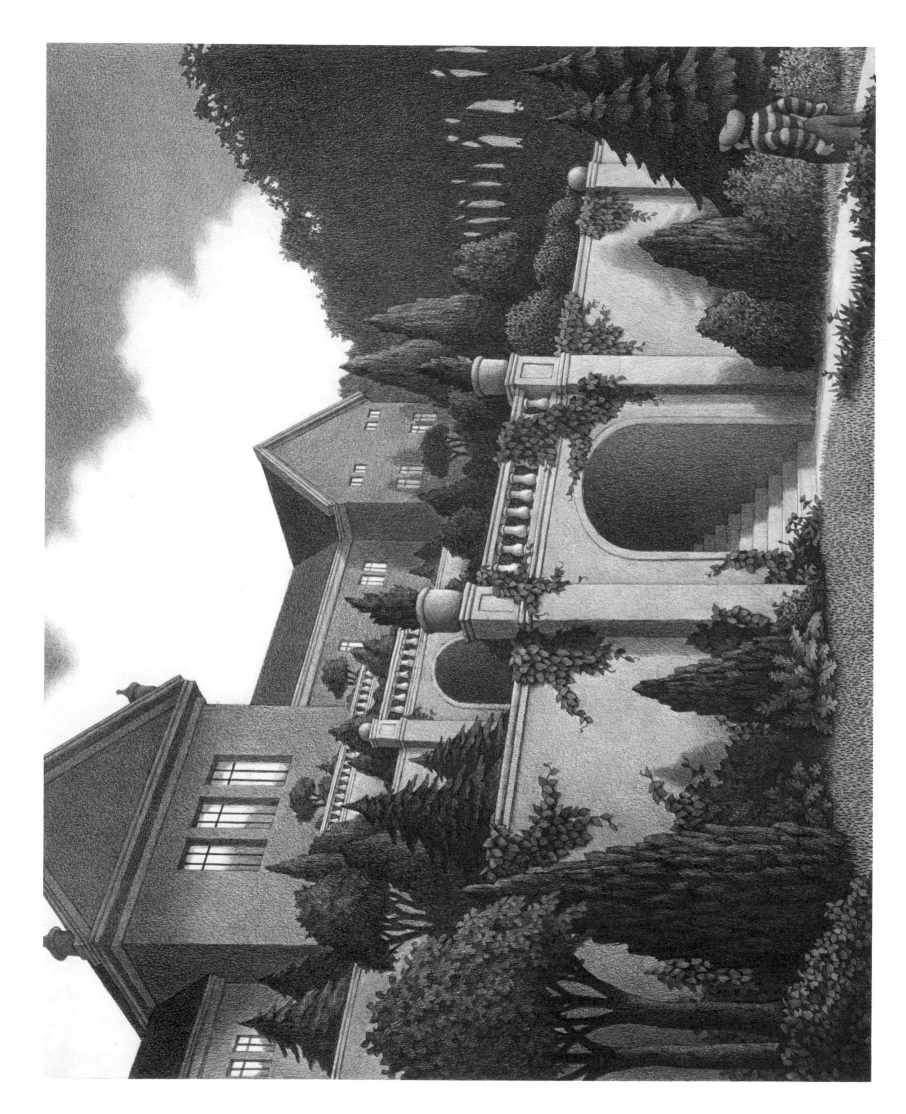

The boy's heart was pounding when he arrived at the huge door. He took a deep breath and reached for the bell, but before he touched it the door swung open. There, in the shadow of the hallway, stood Gasazi the Great. "Greetings, do come in" was all that he said.

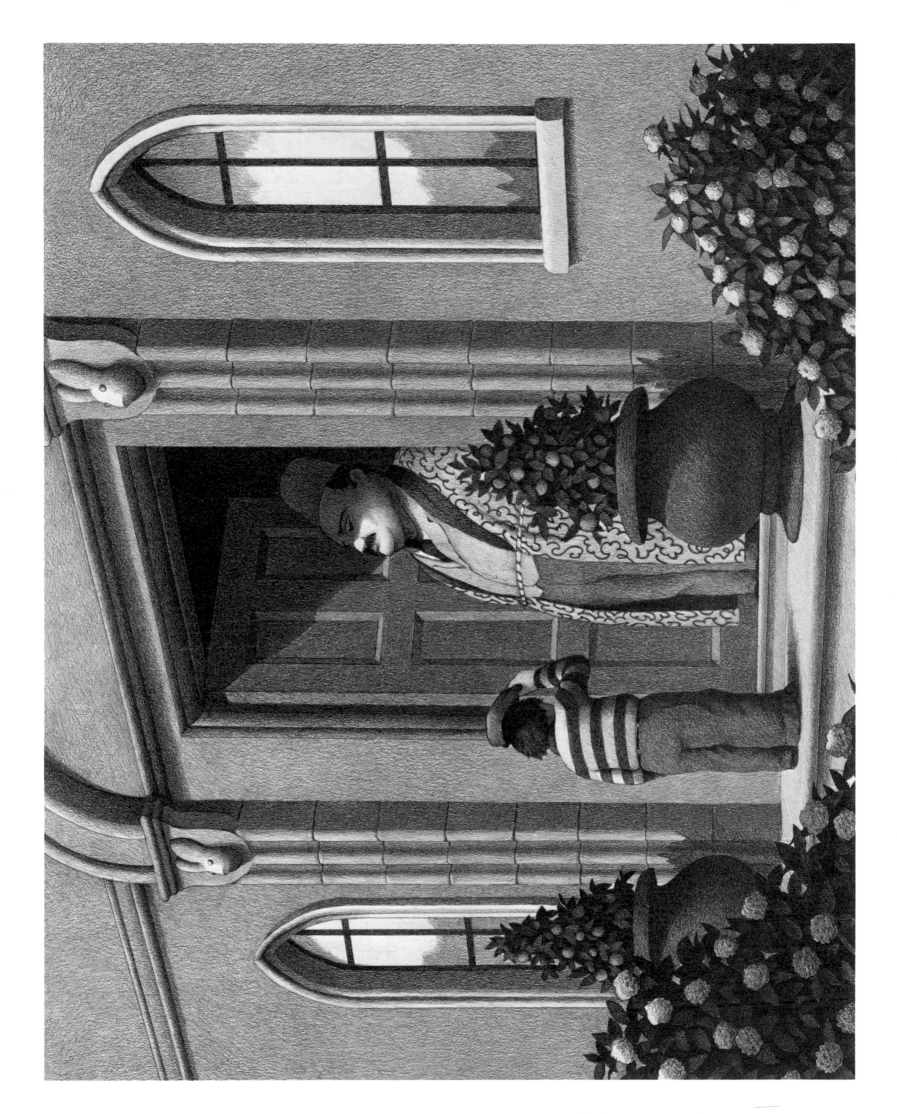

Alan followed Gasazi into a large room. When the magician turned around Alan quickly apologized for letting Fritz into the garden. He politely asked that, if Mr. Gasazi had Fritz, would he please give him back? The magician listened carefully and then, smiling, said, "Certainly you may have your little Fritzie. Follow me." With those words he went to the door and led Alan back outside.

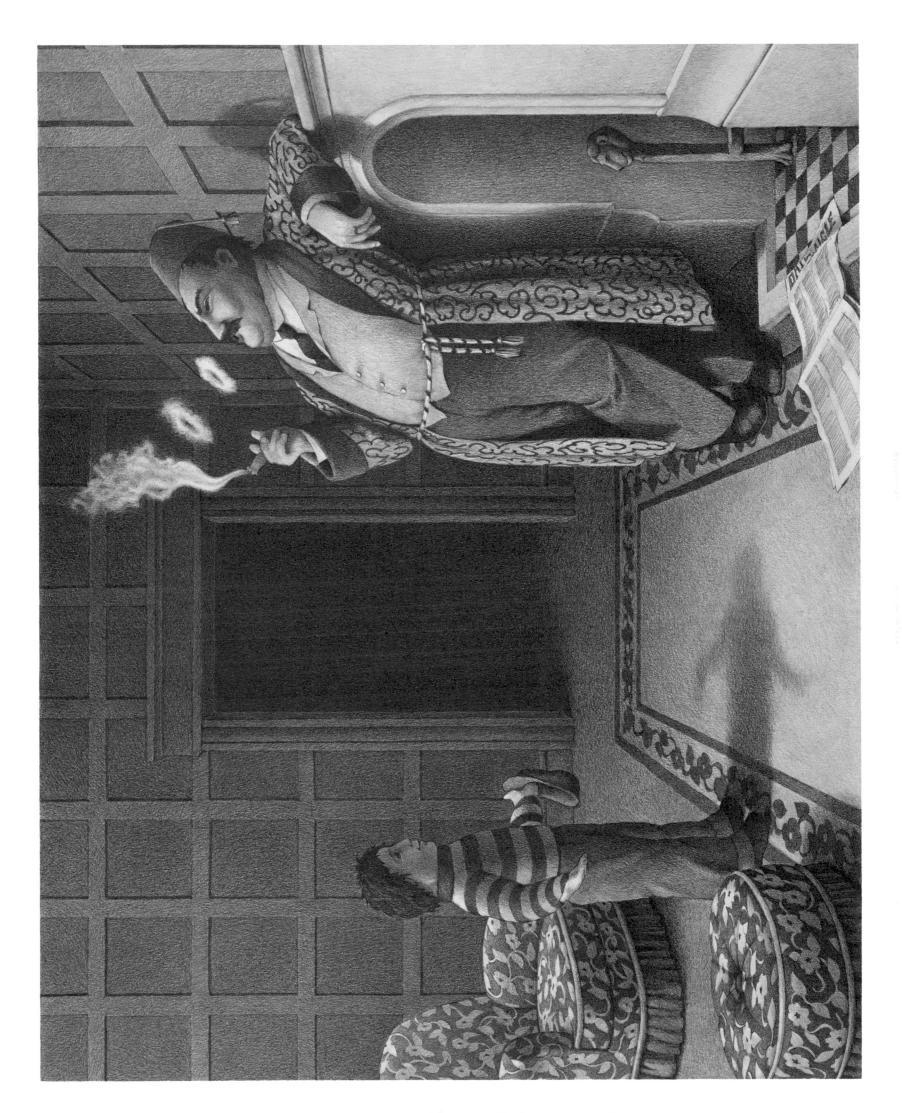

They were walking across the lawn when suddenly Gasazi stopped by a gathering of ducks. He began to speak in a voice that was more like a growl. "I detest dogs. They dig up my flowers, they chew on my trees. Do you know what I do to dogs I find in my garden?" "What?" whispered Alan, almost afraid to hear the answer. "I TURN THEM INTO DUCKS!" bellowed Gasazi. In horror, Alan looked at the birds in front of him. When one duck came forward, Gasazi said, "There's your Fritz." Alan begged the magician to change Fritz back. "Impossible," he answered, "only time can do that. This spell may last years or perhaps just a day. Now take your dear bird and please don't come again."

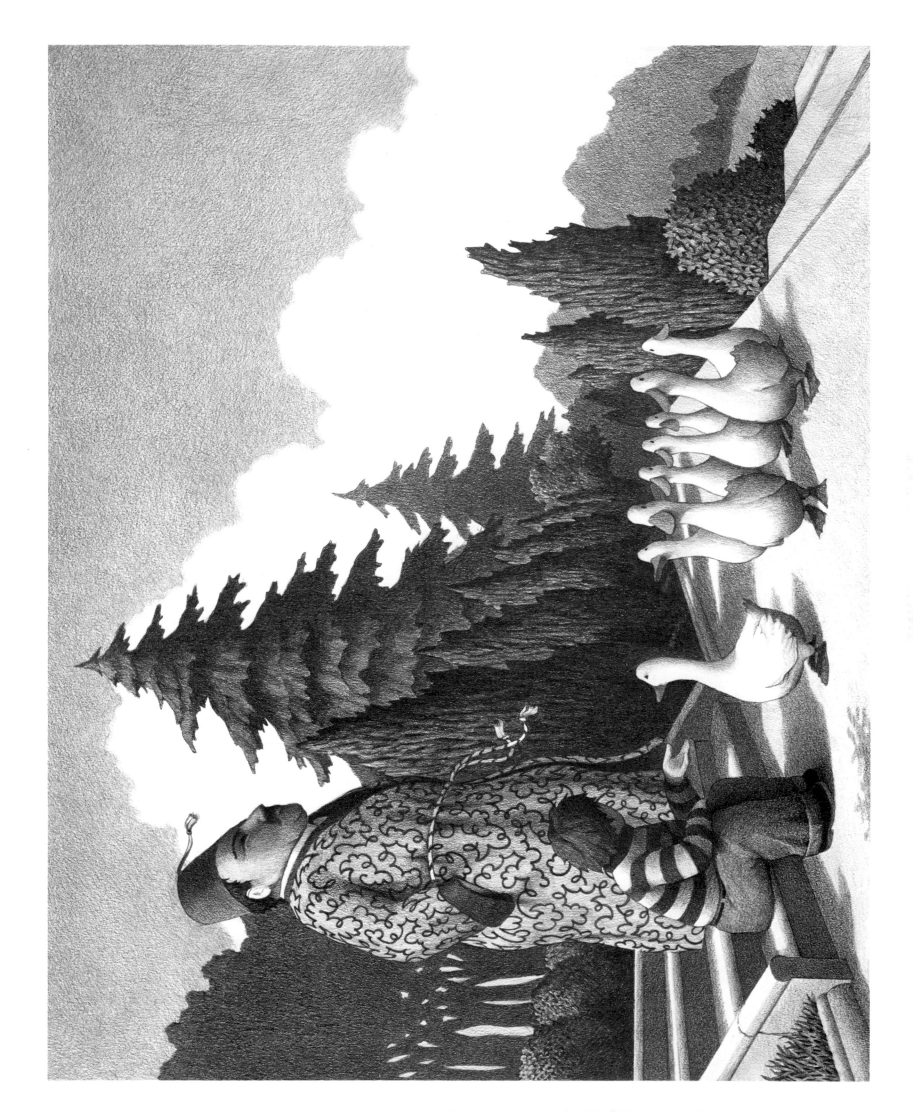

When Alan took the bird in his arms it tried to give him a bite. "Good old boy," said Alan sadly as he patted the bird on the head. "You really haven't changed so much." With tears in his eyes he started for home. Behind him Alan could hear Gasazi laughing. As he approached the stairway, a gust of wind took Alan's hat sailing right off his head. Running along with one arm reaching for the hat, Alan lost his hold on Fritz. The duck flew out ahead and grabbed the hat in midair. But instead of landing he just kept on flying, higher and higher, until he disappeared in the afternoon clouds.

Alan just stood and stared at the empty sky. "Good-bye, old fellow," he called out sadly, sure that Fritz was gone forever. At least he had something to chew on. Slowly, one step after another, Alan found his way back to the garden gate and over the bridge. It was sunset by the time he reached Miss Hester's. Lights were on and he knew she must be home. With a heavy heart he approached the door, wondering how Miss Hester would take the news.

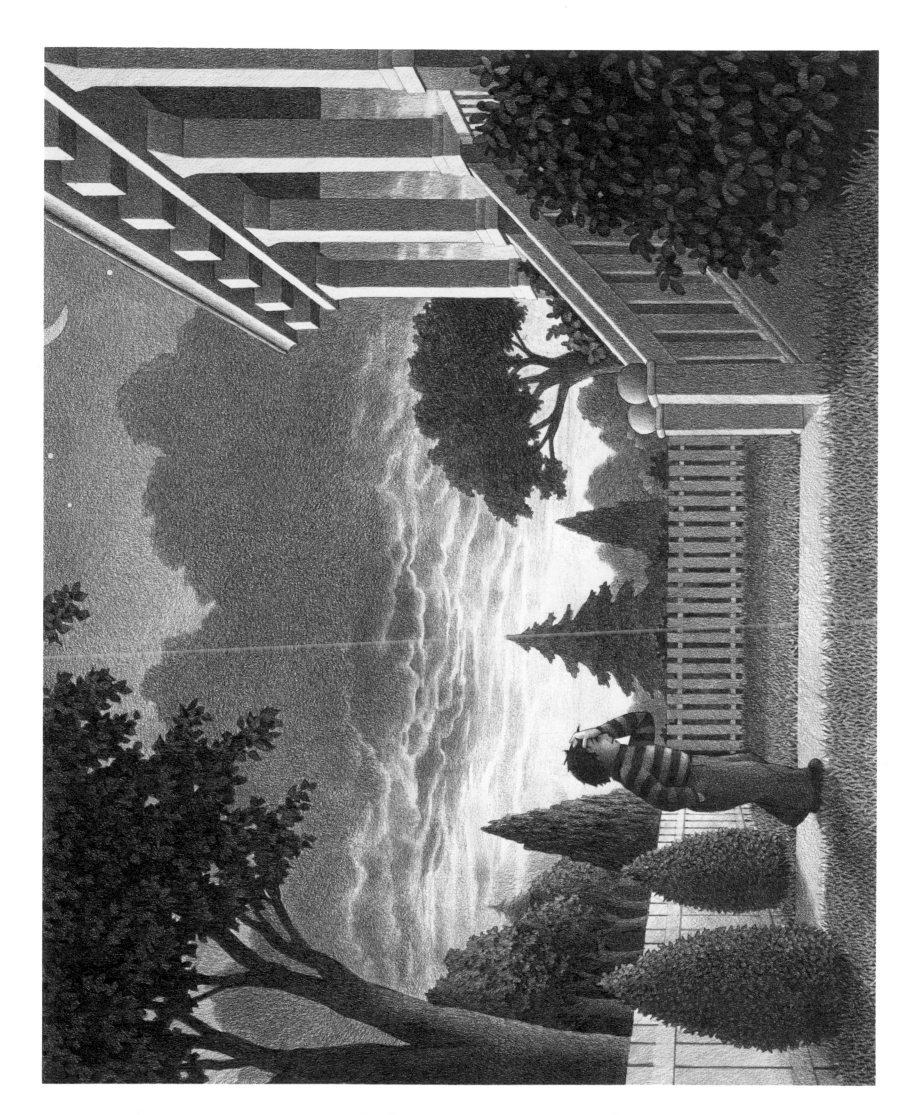

When Miss Hester came to the door Alan blurted out his incredible story. He could barely hold back the tears; then, racing out of the kitchen, dog food on his nose, came Fritz. Alan couldn't believe his eyes. "I'm afraid Mr. Gasazi played a trick on you," said Miss Hester, trying to hide a smile. "Fritz was in the front yard when I returned. He must have found his own way home while you were with Mr. Gasazi. You see, Alan, no one can really turn dogs into ducks; that old magician just made you think that duck was Fritz."

Alan felt very silly. He promised himself he'd never be fooled like that again. He was too old to believe in magic. Miss Hester watched from the porch as Alan waved goodbye and hurried down the road to go home. Then she called out to Fritz, who was playfully running around the front yard. He came trotting up the front steps with something in his mouth and dropped it at Miss Hester's feet. "Why you bad dog," she said. "What are you doing with Alan's hat?"

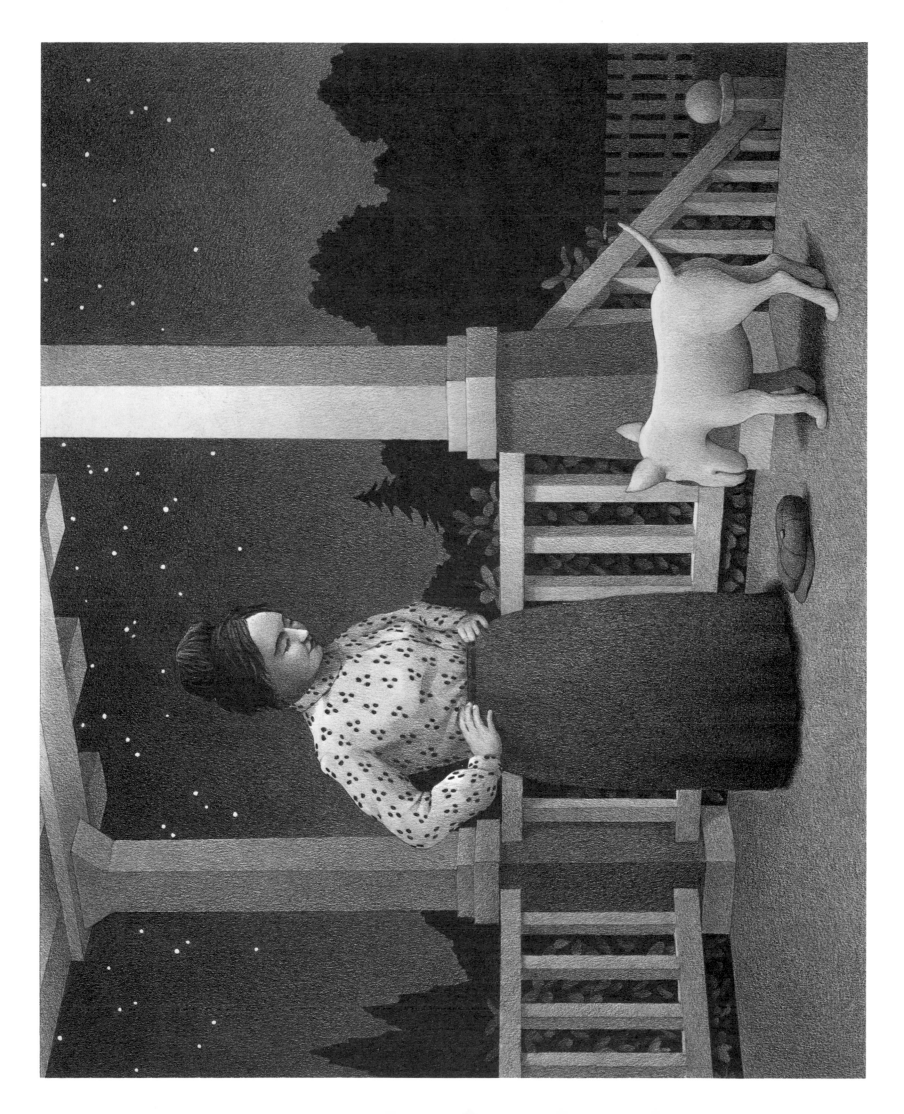